HE WAS THERE
FROM THE DAY WE MOVED IN

STORY BY RHODA LEVINE
DRAWINGS BY EDWARD GOREY

New York Review Books
New York

THIS IS A NEW YORK REVIEW BOOK
PUBLISHED BY THE NEW YORK REVIEW OF BOOKS
435 Hudson Street, New York, NY 10014
www.nyrb.com

Library of Congress Cataloging-in-Publication Data
Levine, Rhoda.
He was there from the day we moved in / by Rhoda Levine ; drawings by Edward Gorey.
p. cm. — (New York Review books children's collection)
Summary: When a family moves into a new house they find a sheep dog in the backyard
that seems to want something, but four-year-old Ogden, his older brother, and their parents
are unable to discover what it is.
ISBN 978-1-59017-515-6 (alk. paper)
[1. Sheep dogs—Fiction. 2. Dogs—Fiction. 3. Family life—Fiction. 4. Names—Fiction.] I.
Gorey, Edward, 1925-2000, ill. II. Title.
PZ7.L5785He 2012
[Fic]—dc23
2011029310

ISBN 978-1-59017-515-6

Cover lettering and design: Rich Tommaso

Printed in the United States on acid-free paper.
1 3 5 7 9 10 8 6 4 2

He was there from the day we moved in. He was there sitting in the garden.

"I wonder if he comes with the yard?" my brother Ogdon asked, as we looked through the window.

"No one mentioned him when we bought the house," my father replied in a puzzled voice. "I wonder what he wants?"

"I think he is waiting for something," I said.

He certainly did look like he was waiting for something, we all agreed.

"He is waiting for *me-e-e!*" my brother Ogdon shouted suddenly, running through the kitchen into the back yard. My brother Ogdon is four.

"I'm sure he is waiting for all of us," my mother insisted, as we followed in Ogdon's footsteps.

We stood there in front of him. He seemed neither pleased nor disappointed to see us.

"Maybe he is waiting for me to jump up and down," my brother Ogdon suggested, jumping up and down.

"Maybe he wants me to do a somersault!" Ogdon had just learned to somersault.

"I know!" breathlessly Ogdon guessed again. "He wants to see me skip on two feet!"

"I think," said my mother, placing a quieting and comforting hand on Ogdon, "he is waiting for something to eat."

My mother is a very practical woman.

I, myself, did not feel that that was the answer. But I watched my mother bring a bowl of milk, a raw hamburger and a soup bone, which she put down in front of him.

Ogdon ran to get a sticky lollypop. It was green! But, after all, Ogdon is only four.

Well, he looked at everything. He gave everything a try—except, of course, the lollypop. I hate green myself.

"He's waiting again!...He is waiting for something else! ...What's he waiting for?" Ogdon was pretty troubled.

"I am sure he is waiting to get to know us," my mother said as she led us indoors. "He just needs to think about us overnight."

Well, that night I certainly thought a lot about him. Of course, I didn't do anything silly like running to the window in my bare feet, to see if he was still there! Ogdon did that.

He was there the next morning. It was raining, but he didn't seem to notice.

My mother smiled. "I'm sure he is waiting to be invited in," she decided. She can never stand to see anyone sitting in the rain.

Well, right away, Ogdon ran out to him. "My mother says c'mon in the house, so c'mon, c'mon!" Nothing happened, so Ogdon ran a line of corn flakes from the door to the dog.

"C'mon, please," he added, quietly.

But he just sat there, his fur dripping, waiting...

The days passed. We fed him. When it got cool, we covered him with a blanket. He didn't seem to mind.

While, all the time, Ogdon tried harder and harder to find out what he was waiting for.

Once Ogdon thought he might want a piece of string.

He tried to bring him a stray cat.

He even tried a box of crayons

...and a calendar.

Ogdon thought he might want to be "talked to."

Do you know, my brother spent a whole afternoon just sitting and talking to him! A whole afternoon is a pretty long time!

Ogdon told me once that he was *sure* he was waiting for a new toy truck.

I really thought that Ogdon was waiting for *that* himself.

When nothing worked, Ogdon began to calm down. Sometimes he didn't talk about him or visit him at all!...Well, it's hard to stay interested in someone who is not interested in you, I don't care how old you are!

I, however, never forgot about him and what he might be waiting for. I never stopped thinking about it—not even when I was asleep, not even when I was playing ball, not even when I was reading.

Well, one night, I guess I was thinking harder than usual. I had been studying him as he sat in the moonlight with his eyes closed. "Listen," I thought, "you've got food, friends, a home. What is it you *really* want?"

Well, suddenly, I knew, just like that. He wanted a name! *He was waiting for a name!*

The next morning I started a list. I wrote down every name I had ever heard. I looked for names in all the books we owned. I even looked on trucks and posters! Not that I intended to call him MATT'S MACHINE SHOP or ACME WRECKING or anything like that. I just wanted to get up a good store of possibilities.

Naming a grownup dog is not like naming a baby, you know. You have to find the exact one that suits him, the one he has been waiting for. You can't jump into a name just like that!

By dinner time, I had the longest list I had ever seen—and very interesting too—with the best names traced over in fountain pen.

"What are you drawing?" Ogdon asked. My brother Ogdon can't read.

"I'm not drawing," I said. "I'm writing."

"What are you writing?"

That's when I made my big mistake. I told Ogdon what I was writing, and why. Ogdon's eyes grew wide when I told him. Sometimes he thinks I am pretty smart. His eyes got so wide that I didn't notice: he was backing up while I talked.

Suddenly he was gone! He was running toward the back yard yelling, "I know, *I know his name!*" He was in the yard before I could stop him. Sometimes four-year-olds can run faster than anyone.

"Wait," I cried, "you've got to think before—" But I guess he just couldn't stop. I was sort of glad my parents were doing the dishes so they didn't have to see what happened.

Ogdon ran right up to him, stopped short and pointed at his nose. "Your name!—" Ogdon was breathless. "Your name, *I know your name!* It's—" He lifted up an ear and whispered into it. Then he stepped back.

I have never seen Ogdon look so proud and happy!

We didn't breathe for a whole minute. That dog just blinked. Then, slowly, he looked up with sad and patient eyes. He blinked again, like he was giving it a second thought. Then he stood up, shook himself, and began to walk—like he was old and tired—toward the end of the garden.

Well, when Ogdon told me the name he whispered, I must say that I would have walked away too. Well, whoever heard of naming a dog "Marilyn"—even if it is the name of the girl who used to live next door!

I thought Ogdon was pretty dumb, but I didn't tell him. He looked so sad standing there. I mean *really* sad!

I guess it was the way that Ogdon looked that made me do it. Suddenly I took off after that dog. I got right in front of him and started talking.

He kept padding along . . .

"Listen," I said, "I've got a list of possible names you haven't heard yet! Names like Bouncer, Arthur, George and Garson— "

He stopped walking . . .

He blinked.

"Oh, I know they may not be the right names," I added quickly, "but I've got others. French names, names of places, adjectives and everything. Well, you've just got to give me a chance!"

He shook himself.

"Listen, my father told me that a dog is man's best friend. Well, friends don't walk out on people because of one bad guess. Friends give people a second chance, you know!"

I think that's what got him! He blinked again . . . and then he sat down.

Well, he is still sitting and waiting. He is closer to the garden's edge, but he is still there.

Ogdon hugs him a lot, though he doesn't say much to him.

You know, I think we're bound to find the right name sooner or later. I, myself, am still working on the whole thing. He is waiting; I am thinking. We're both trying.

And, like my mother always says, that's about the best anyone can do. . .

RHODA LEVINE is the author of seven children's books (two of which were illustrated by Edward Gorey) and is an accomplished director and choreographer. In addition to working for major opera houses in the United States and Europe, she has choreographed shows on and off Broadway, and in London's West End. Among the world premieres she has directed are *Der Kaiser von Atlantis*, by Viktor Ullmann, and *The Life and Times of Malcolm X* and *Wakonda's Dream*, both by Anthony Davis. In Cape Town she directed the South African premiere of *Porgy and Bess* in 1996, and she premiered the New York City Opera productions of Janacek's *From the House of the Dead*, Zimmermann's *Die Soldaten*, and Adamo's *Little Women*.

Levine has taught acting and improvisation at the Yale School of Drama, the Curtis Institute of Music, and Northwestern University, and is currently on the faculty of the Manhattan School of Music and the Mannes College of Music. She lives in New York, where she is the artistic director of the city's only improvisational opera company, Play It by Ear.

EDWARD GOREY (1925–2000) was born in Chicago. He studied briefly at the Art Institute of Chicago, spent three years in the army testing poison gas, and attended Harvard College, where he majored in French literature and roomed with the poet Frank O'Hara. In 1953 Gorey published *The Unstrung Harp*, the first of his many extraordinary books, which include *The Curious Sofa*, *The Haunted Tea-Cosy*, and *The Epileptic Bicycle*. In addition to illustrating his own books, Gorey provided drawings to countless books for both children and adults. Of these, New York Review Books has published *The Haunted Looking Glass*, a collection of Gothic tales that he selected and illustrated; *The War of the Worlds*, the pioneering work of science fiction by H. G. Wells; *Men and Gods*, a retelling of ancient Greek myths by Rex Warner; and *Three Ladies Beside the Sea*, an earlier collaboration with Rhoda Levine.

TITLES IN
THE NEW YORK REVIEW CHILDREN'S COLLECTION

EILÍS DILLON
The Island of Horses
The Lost Island

ELEANOR FARJEON
The Little Bookroom

PENELOPE FARMER
Charlotte Sometimes

RUMER GODDEN
An Episode of Sparrows
The Mousewife

LUCRETIA P. HALE
The Peterkin Papers

RUSSELL and LILLIAN HOBAN
The Sorely Trying Day

RUTH KRAUSS and MARC SIMONT
The Backward Day

MUNRO LEAF and ROBERT LAWSON
Wee Gillis

RHODA LEVINE and EDWARD GOREY
Three Ladies Beside the Sea

BETTY JEAN LIFTON and EIKOH-HOSOE
Taka-chan and I

NORMAN LINDSAY
The Magic Pudding

ERIC LINKLATER
The Wind on the Moon

J. P. MARTIN
Uncle
Uncle Cleans Up

JOHN MASEFIELD
The Box of Delights
The Midnight Folk

E. NESBIT
The House of Arden

DANIEL PINKWATER
Lizard Music

ALASTAIR REID and BOB GILL
Supposing…

ALASTAIR REID and BEN SHAHN
Ounce Dice Trice

BARBARA SLEIGH
Carbonel and Calidor
Carbonel: The King of the Cats
The Kingdom of Carbonel

E. C. SPYKMAN
Terrible, Horrible Edie

FRANK TASHLIN
The Bear That Wasn't